Paint the Elephant

Amanda Elise Lechner

With deep gratitude to my
wonderful family and friends.
For you and because of you.

Paint the Elephant loved three things in life: eating pancakes, painting pictures, and playing with his pals.

Every morning, he woke up early to eat a pancake breakfast before going out to play with his pals.

At 12:00 PM sharp, he would head home to eat pancakes for lunch.

At dinner time, he ate extra fluffy pancakes with extra butter and extra syrup.

At night time, he ate pancakes in his dreams.

One day, Paint felt very sick. His tummy hurt a lot. He did not want to eat pancakes. He did not want to paint pictures. He did not want to play with his pals.

He went to see Dr. Benjamin George, and Dr. Benjamin George took x-rays of his stomach. The x-rays revealed some very bad news.

"Paint," Dr. Benjamin George said. "I think I know what's wrong with your stomach."

"What could it be?"

"Well, I think you've been eating too many pancakes."

"Oh," said Paint. "That's about all I eat."

"I see," said Dr. Benjamin George. Then he said, "Here's your medicine. Eat vegetables. Lots of them. Everyday. Lay off the pancakes for a while. Your tummy will feel a lot better."

Paint was very sad to hear that he had to eat vegetables. He cried all the way home.

When Paint made it home, he kept crying. He just did not know how he was going to stop eating pancakes. Even worse, he did not know how he would eat vegetables!

Then Paint remembered: whenever you have to do something that's just too hard, call a pal to help.

So Paint called his very best pal from kindergarten, Jeremy the Skunk. "I need your help," Paint said.

Remembering all the times Paint had been right by his side, Jeremy said, "Of course, Paint. Anything for my dear pal. What do you need?"

"The doctor said I need to stop eating pancakes for a while. I need to eat vegetables instead."

"Oh my," Jeremy said, knowing just how hard this would be. "It's going to be okay," he said. "How many vegetables do you have to eat?"

"A lot," Paint said.

"Today?" asked Jeremy.

"Everyday," Paint said.

"Then we will probably need some more pals to help. We will probably need a pal for Monday, Tuesday, Wednesday, Thursday, Friday, Saturday, and Sunday. That means we will need seven pals — well six pals, plus me," said Jeremy. He was always very good at math.

"Good idea," said Paint. He felt a little better knowing he had his very best pal to help him through this very hard time.

Paint called August the Polar Bear and said, "Hi August, it's Paint. I need a favor." Recalling that Paint had helped him repair his roof last winter, August said, "Sure thing, pal." Paint now had two pals to help.

Next Paint called his old pal, Halley the Cat. Remembering the many times that Paint had come over in the middle of the night to help her look for monsters under the bed, Halley said, "Of course I'll help." Paint now had three pals to help.

He called his dear pal, Lauren the Dog. "Lauren, it's Paint," he said. "I need your help."

Thinking about the time last summer when Paint had stayed at her house for a week to take care of her fish while she was out of town, Lauren said, "Of course, Paint. Anything for you. What can I do?"

Paint now had four pals to help.

Next Paint called Jeana the Owl and Nikki the Turtle. Jeana thought of the time when Paint had helped her plant a beautiful garden in her backyard and felt very excited for the chance to help her pal. Nikki, forever grateful to Paint for teaching her how to surf a few summers back, was delighted to help. Paint now had six friends to help.

Paint called Ryan the Sloth. Ryan would never forget how Paint had helped him move to a new house on a very hot day in the middle of the summer, and so he happily agreed to help, too.

Paint now had seven friends to help. He was so happy that he forgot to be sad about missing pancakes (but just for a minute).

On Monday, Jeremy came over to Paint's house with celery. Like Paint, he did not want to eat vegetables, but he agreed to eat them with his pal. On the count of three, they each took a bite. Together they found out that celery tastes pretty good!

On Tuesday, August came over with butternut squash soup. "Vegetables can be soup?" Paint asked. "They sure can," said August. Paint actually kind of liked soup even though it is not pancakes, and he especially liked August's butternut squash soup.

On Wednesday, Halley brought spinach. Paint was a little scared of how it looked, but he trusted his pal enough to take a bite. He could not believe that spinach does not taste gross, so he took another bite. Upon his second bite, he was convinced that spinach actually tastes very good.

On Thursday, Lauren came over to Paint's house with beets. She herself was a big vegetable eater, so she was actually very glad to share this meal with her pal. Paint watched her eat first, and then he asked her to hold his hand while he took a bite. You know what he learned? Beets are all right!

On Friday, Jeana brought over brussel sprouts. Paint was starting to like vegetables more and more. Together, they enjoyed a delicious dinner.

On Saturday, Nikki brought carrots. Paint was excited to try an orange vegetable and very glad to find out that carrots are quite a treat.

On Sunday, Ryan did not show up at Paint's house. Paint was so sad that he almost started to cry. He then almost ate pancakes even though he was not supposed to, but instead he decided it probably made more sense to call Ryan.

"Hey pal. Do you think you can still come over today to eat vegetables with me?" Paint asked.

"Why don't you come to my house, Paint?" Ryan asked. So Paint walked down the block to Ryan's house. Then the best thing happened.

All of Paint's pals were at Ryan's house, and together they had a party to celebrate Paint's big accomplishment: one whole week full of vegetables — without any pancakes.

Paint the Elephant, who just one week earlier had no idea how he would ever recover from the loss of pancakes, was very thankful for his dear pals.

"I couldn't have done it without you," he said. "Now I know that, with a little help from my pals, I can do anything."

Color your own party with Paint and his pals!

Amanda Elise Lechner is an author and illustrator of children's books, including *Paint the Elephant* and *Rainbow the Magic Butterfly*. She lives in Northern California with her family and finds inspiration for her art and writing from the natural beauty of the Golden State. Her books are available on Amazon.

Made in the USA
Lexington, KY
07 December 2019